For all the storytellers
of Toronto, young and old.
C.L.

To Maryanne, Joanne and Theo
with gratitude.
And to Stephen Gammell and Cynthia Rylant
who unwittingly sowed the seed.
I.W.

Special thanks to the staff of the
Metropolitan Toronto Reference Library,
circulating picture collection.

Text copyright © 1989 by Celia Barker Lottridge
Illustrations copyright © 1989 by Ian Wallace
Ninth printing 2013

Groundwood Books / House of Anansi Press
110 Spadina Avenue, Suite 801, Toronto, Ontario M5V 2K4

Distributed in the USA by Publishers Group West
1700 Fourth Street, Berkeley, CA 94710

We acknowledge for their financial support of our publishing program
the Canada Council for the Arts, the Government of Canada through
the Canada Book Fund (CBF) and the Ontario Arts Council.

Canada Council   Conseil des Arts   ONTARIO ARTS COUNCIL
for the Arts   du Canada   CONSEIL DES ARTS DE L'ONTARIO

Library and Archives Canada Cataloging in Publication
Lottridge, Celia B. (Celia Barker)
The name of the tree
ISBN-13 978-0-88899-097-6
I. Wallace, Ian II. Title.
PS8573.087N35 1989 jC813'.54 C89-093426-6
PZ7.L67Na 1989

Design by Michael Solomon
Printed and bound in China by
Everbest Printing Co. Ltd.

THE NAME OF THE TREE

A BANTU TALE RETOLD BY Celia Barker Lottridge
AND ILLUSTRATED BY Ian Wallace

GROUNDWOOD BOOKS   HOUSE OF ANANSI PRESS   TORONTO   BERKELEY

NCE, long ago, in the land of the short grass, there was a great hunger. No rain fell, and no grass grew.

The ostrich, the gazelle, the giraffe, the monkey, the rabbit, the tortoise, the zebra, and all the other animals were hungry. They searched in the jungle, they searched by the river, they searched on the great flat plain, but they could find nothing to eat.

At last all the animals gathered together and they said, "Let us go together across the great flat plain until we come to something we can eat."

And so all the animals, except for the lion, who was king and lived in the jungle, walked across the flat, empty land. They walked and walked. After many days, they saw a small bump on the edge of the flat land.

Then they saw that the small bump was a tree.

And the tree was very tall.

And the tree had fruit on it, such fruit as they had never seen before.

It was as red as pomegranates, as yellow as bananas, as green as melons, as purple as plums, as orange as mangos, and it smelled like all the fruits of the world.

But the tree was so tall and the branches so high that even the giraffe couldn't reach the fruit. And the trunk was so smooth that even the monkey couldn't climb the tree.

The animals sat on the ground and cried because the fruit smelled so good and they were so hungry.

At last, when they were too tired to cry any longer, a very old tortoise spoke.

"O animals," she said, "my great-great-great-grandmother told me a story about a wonderful tree. The fruit of that tree was delicious and good to eat. But it could be reached only by those who knew the name of the tree."

The animals cried out, "But who can tell us the name of the tree?"

The very old tortoise answered, "The king knows. We must send someone to ask him."

"I will go," said the gazelle. "I am the fastest runner of us all." And that was true.

So the gazelle started out across the great flat plain. He ran like an arrow shot from a bow, and as he ran he thought, "How lucky the animals are that I am willing to go to the king. No one can run as fast as I."

Indeed, it was not long before the gazelle reached the jungle and the place by the river where the king lived.

The king was sitting with his tail neatly wrapped around him. Every hair in his golden coat lay smooth and shining. He spoke kindly to the gazelle. "What do you wish of me?" he said.

"O great king," said the gazelle, "all the animals are hungry and we have found a tree filled with wonderful fruit. But we cannot eat the fruit until we know the name of the tree."

"I will tell you," said the lion, "but you must remember, for I don't want to have to tell anyone else. The name of the tree is Ungalli."

"Ungalli," said the gazelle. "I will run as fast as the wind and I will reach the tree before I can possibly forget."

The gazelle thanked the king and began to run through the jungle and across the great flat plain. He thought about how happy all the animals would be, and how they would thank him and be grateful to him. He thought about this so hard that he did not see a rabbit hole that lay in his path, not far from where the animals were waiting. He stepped in it and went head over hoofs over head over hoofs. He landed in a heap at the foot of the tree.

"What is the name of the tree?" shouted the animals.

The gazelle shook his head. He shook it again. But the name was gone. "I can't remember," he whispered.

The animals groaned. "We will have to send someone else," they said. "Someone who will not forget."

"I will go," said the elephant. "I never forget anything."

The animals nodded, for this was true. And so the elephant strode off across the great flat plain.

"I will not forget," she said to herself. "I can remember anything I choose to. Even the names of all my cousins." The elephant had hundreds of cousins. "Or the names of all the stars in the sky."

When the elephant arrived at the edge of the river, the king was sitting in his usual place, but the end of his tail was twitching and his fur was ruffled.

"What do you want?" he growled.

"O king," said the elephant, "all the animals are hungry…"

"I know," said the lion, "and you want to know the name of the tree with the wonderful fruit. I will tell you, but don't you forget because I absolutely will not tell anyone else. The name of the tree is Ungalli."

"I will not forget," said the elephant haughtily. "I never forget anything." And she turned and began to make her way out of the jungle.

"Forget," she grumbled to herself. "Me, forget! Why, I can remember the names of all the trees in this jungle." And she began to name them. When she had finished the jungle trees, she went on to all the other trees in Africa. She was just starting on the trees of the rest of the world when she happened to step in the very rabbit hole that had tripped the gazelle. Her foot fitted exactly into the hole, so exactly that she couldn't get it out.

The animals waiting under the tree saw the elephant and ran toward her calling, "What is the name of the tree?"

The elephant pulled and tugged and pulled and tugged, and at last with a great *pop* her foot came out of the hole.

"I can't remember," she said crossly, "and I don't care. That tree has caused far too much trouble already."

The animals didn't even groan. They were too tired and too hungry.

After a long time a very young tortoise spoke.

"O animals," he said, "I will go and find out the name of the tree."

"You!" said the animals. "But you are so young and you are so small and you are so slow."

"Yes," said the very young tortoise. "But I know how to remember. I learned from my great-great-great-grandmother, the one who told you about the tree."

The animals had nothing to say. And the little tortoise was already on his way. It is true that he was slow. But by putting one short leg ahead of the other he crossed the great flat plain, went through the jungle, and arrived at the place by the river where the king lived.

The king was not sitting in his usual place. He was pacing up and down the bank of the river, waving his tail. His fur was standing on end.

When he saw the very young tortoise, he roared, "If you have come to ask me the name of the tree, go home. I have told the gazelle and I have told the elephant and I will *not* tell you that the name of the tree is Ungalli."

The very young tortoise nodded his head politely. He turned and began to walk out of the jungle.

As he walked he said, "Ungalli, Ungalli, the name of the tree is Ungalli. Ungalli, Ungalli, the name of the tree is Ungalli."

And he went on saying it as he crossed the great flat plain. "Ungalli, Ungalli, the name of the tree is Ungalli."

And he never stopped saying it, even when he got tired, even when he got thirsty. Because that is what his great-great-great-grandmother had told him to do. Even when he fell right to the bottom of that same rabbit hole, the very young tortoise just climbed out saying, "Ungalli, Ungalli, the name of the tree is Ungalli."

None of the animals saw him coming. They were sitting under the tree, looking at the ground. The very young tortoise walked straight up to the foot of the tree and said in a loud voice, "The name of the tree is Ungalli!"

The animals looked up.

They saw the branches of the tree bend down so low that they could reach the wonderful fruit that was as red as pomegranates, as yellow as bananas, as green as melons, as purple as plums, and as orange as mangos, and smelled like all the fruits of the world.

The animals ate. They ate until they could eat no more. And then they lifted the very young tortoise high in the air and marched around the tree chanting, "Ungalli, Ungalli, the name of the tree is Ungalli," because they did not want to forget. And they never did.